Dear Parents:

Congratulations! Your child is taking the first steps on an exciting journey. The destination? Independent reading!

STEP INTO READING® will help your child get there. The program offers five steps to reading success. Each step includes fun stories and colorful art or photographs. In addition to original fiction and books with favorite characters, there are Step into Reading Non-Fiction Readers, Phonics Readers and Boxed Sets, Sticker Readers, and Comic Readers—a complete literacy program with something to interest every child.

Learning to Read, Step by Step!

Ready to Read   Preschool–Kindergarten
• big type and easy words • rhyme and rhythm • picture clues
For children who know the alphabet and are eager to begin reading.

Reading with Help   Preschool–Grade 1
• basic vocabulary • short sentences • simple stories
For children who recognize familiar words and sound out new words with help.

Reading on Your Own   Grades 1–3
• engaging characters • easy-to-follow plots • popular topics
For children who are ready to read on their own.

Reading Paragraphs   Grades 2–3
• challenging vocabulary • short paragraphs • exciting stories
For newly independent readers who read simple sentences with confidence.

Ready for Chapters   Grades 2–4
• chapters • longer paragraphs • full-color art
For children who want to take the plunge into chapter books but still like colorful pictures.

STEP INTO READING® is designed to give every child a successful reading experience. The grade levels are only guides; children will progress through the steps at their own speed, developing confidence in their reading.

Remember, a lifetime love of reading starts with a single step!

created by

Step into Reading, Random House, and the Random House colophon are registered trademarks of Random House LLC.

Visit us on the Web!
StepIntoReading.com
randomhousekids.com

Educators and librarians, for a variety of teaching tools, visit us at RHTeachersLibrarians.com

ISBN 978-0-385-38773-6 (trade) — ISBN 978-0-385-38774-3 (lib. bdg.)

Printed in the United States of America
10 9 8 7 6 5 4 3 2

nickelodeon

THE SPONGEBOB MOVIE
SPONGE OUT OF WATER

Food Fight!

adapted by Courtney Carbone
illustrated by Dave Aikins

Random House 🏠 New York

SpongeBob is a cook.
He makes
Krabby Patties.

He uses
a top-secret recipe!

Mr. Krabs locks
the Krabby Patty recipe
in a safe.

Plankton is planning
to steal the recipe!

7

Look!

Plankton flies over

the Krusty Krab.

He drops a giant jar
of tartar sauce.
It's a food fight!

SpongeBob and Patrick
must defend
the Krusty Krab!
SpongeBob tells Patrick
to load the potatoes.

"Mashed?" asks Patrick.

"Raw!" says SpongeBob.

The potatoes hit
Plankton's plane.
The plane slices them
into french fries!

THE
KRUSTY
KRAB

Fries rain down.

The crowd cheers!

SpongeBob and Patrick

do a happy dance.

But the fight
is not over.
Plankton has a tank!

Plankton launches pickles!
A pickle blows the roof off the Krusty Krab!

SpongeBob and Patrick
fire ketchup, mustard,
and mayo at the tank.

The tank explodes.

Boom!

Plankton will not give up.

He is wearing

a giant robot suit!

Oh, no!

Plankton breaks a wall
in the Krusty Krab!

Plankton reaches

for the secret recipe!

SpongeBob gasps.

Mr. Krabs groans.

The robot stops!

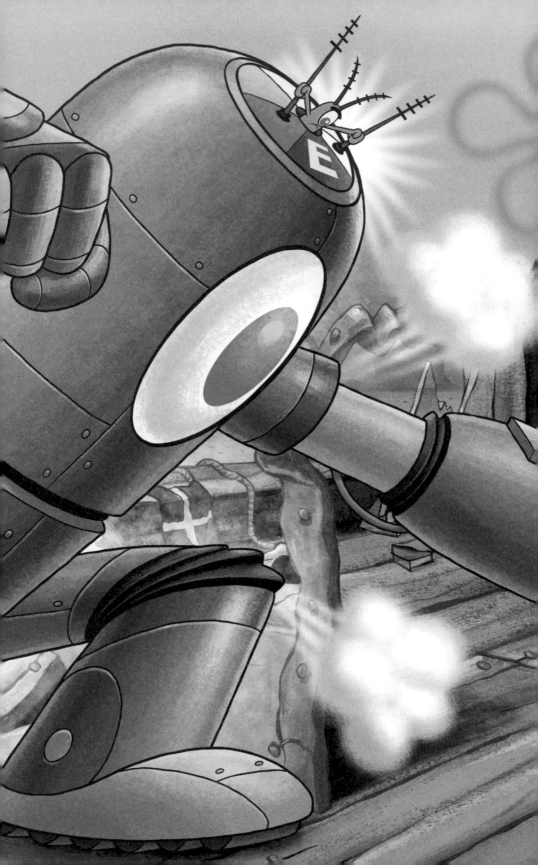

The robot is out of gas.
It cannot reach
the recipe!

Plankton walks away.
The Krabby Patty
recipe is safe!